Hal the Highwayman

Written by June Crebbin

Illustrated by Polly Dunbar

WALKER BOOKS

AND SUBSIDIARIES

LONDON · BOSTON · SYDNEY

Hal was a highwayman.
At dead of night, when the wind
was howling through the trees and
the rain swept across the moors,
he went riding, riding, riding.
But he wasn't very good.

Sometimes he fell off his horse into the duck pond.

Sometimes he got
caught up in a tree.

When the moon lit up the sky like a giant lantern, Hal waited for a stagecoach to come by.

But he wasn't very good.
Often he waited at
the wrong place.

He tried to look fierce.
But no one was frightened of him.

Then, one day, he saw an advertisement in "Robbers' Weekly".

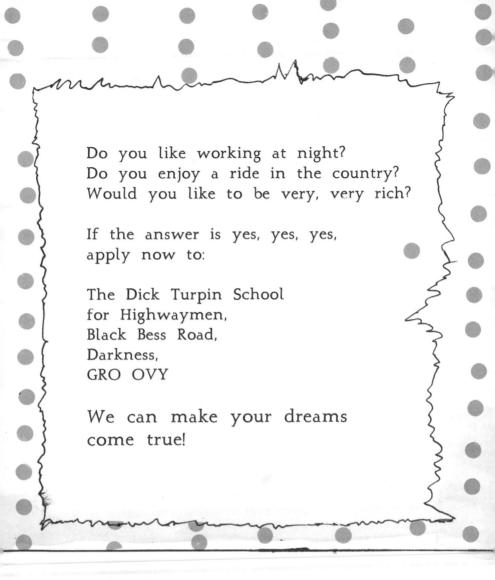

Do you like working at night?
Do you enjoy a ride in the country?
Would you like to be very, very rich?

If the answer is yes, yes, yes,
apply now to:

The Dick Turpin School
for Highwaymen,
Black Bess Road,
Darkness,
GRO OVY

We can make your dreams
come true!

Hal wrote off at once.

Dear Dick,
   I would like to be a
highwayman like you but
I think I need a few lessons.
Please may I come to your
school?
      Yours hopefully,
      Hal 🙂
PS How long is the course?

A reply came within a few days.

Dear Hal,
    Come at once.
I enclose a kit list.
    Yours,

Dick Turpin

    Dick Turpin
PS About a week.

Hal read the kit list.

The Dick Turpin School for Highwaymen

Kit List

You will need:

1. Horse — mostly black.

2. Boots —

   shiny black.

Then he packed his bags …

3. Cloak –

long, black.

4. Hat – wide brim, black.

5. Piece of cloth or leather –

definitely black.

and set off for the school.

First he had riding lessons.
He learnt jumping ...

galloping ...

and how to stand
perfectly still in
the shadows.

He studied maps.

Dead
Man's
Pass

Fearful
Forest

LONELY MOOR

Roaring River

Stinking Swamp

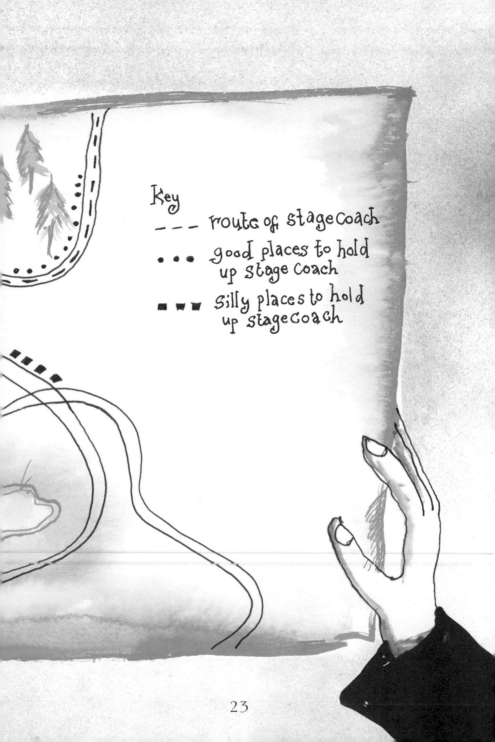

Key

--- route of stage coach

••• good places to hold
up stage coach

■■■ Silly places to hold
up stage coach

He learnt how to make a mask.

After one week, he had a report:

The Dick Turpin
School for Highwaymen

Progress Report

Name: Hal

Riding: Could do better. Hal must remember to ride slowly when going downhill, and lean backwards not forwards.

Map work: Could do better. Hal must always check the route the stagecoach is taking.

Shouting: Could do better. Hal must imagine he is a giant, not a mouse.

Mask-making: Could do better. Hal must remember to cut eye-holes in the mask so he can see where he is going.

General: Could do better.

Signed: Dick Turpin

Hal had more lessons ... and more lessons. He learnt how to jump OVER a duck pond ...

and duck UNDER
the trees.

He knew how to read a map.

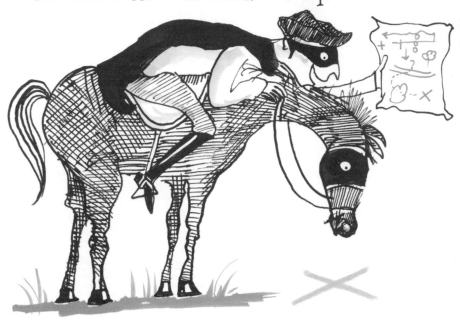

His mask was perfect.

After six weeks, Hal had his final report. At last it was a good one.

"And remember," said Dick Turpin as he said goodbye, "never, never, NEVER go out without your mask!"

The very next night, a stagecoach
carrying a tailor, a cobbler and
a hatter sped over the moor.
Near the crossroads, hidden in
the trees, Hal waited until the
stagecoach was almost upon him.
Then out he sprang.

33

The tailor, the cobbler and the hatter
tumbled out of the coach and
handed over their money.
Off Hal galloped.

The following day, Hal rode into town
to spend the money.
In the first shop, he chose some cloth
for a new suit.
"Don't I know you?" asked the tailor.
"Of course not," said Hal.

In the second shop, he admired
a pair of shiny black boots.
"Haven't I seen you somewhere
before?" asked the cobbler.
"Don't be silly," said Hal.

In the third shop, Hal tried on a black
top hat.
"Didn't I see you last night?" asked
the hatter.
Hal was looking at himself in the mirror.

"Doesn't this hat go well with my mask?" he said.

"You're the highwayman!" shouted the tailor, the cobbler and the hatter.

Hal gasped and sprang to the door...

But the tailor, the cobbler and the hatter grabbed him by his coat tails and hung on.

"OUR money or YOUR life!" they
shouted.
Hal wriggled out of his coat and
ran for it.

At home, Hal sank into his armchair.
All that trouble, he thought, and still
I'm not rich. Being a highwayman
is too much like
hard work.

He picked up his latest "Robbers'
Weekly". On the front page was
an advertisement.

Do you want to sail the seas?
Do you enjoy singing sea songs?
Would you like to be very, very rich?

If the answer is yes, yes, yes,
apply now to:

Captain Blackbeard School
for Pirates,
Salt Lane,
Seaside,
Devon,
CO OL

We can make your dreams
come true!

A life on

"A life on the ocean wave," sang Hal,
   as he rode into town to buy a parrot.
"A pirate's life for me! Yo ho!"

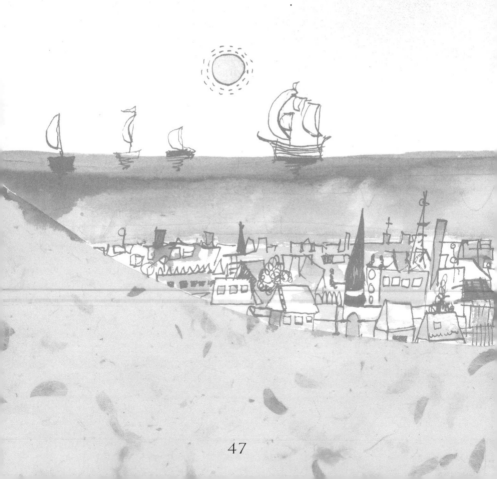

For John Robert Mark
J.C.
For Lewis Wilson
P.D.

Walker Starters

The Dragon Test by June Crebbin, illustrated by Polly Dunbar
0-7445-9018-3
Hal the Highwayman by June Crebbin, illustrated by Polly Dunbar
0-7445-9019-1
Cup Run by Martin Waddell, illustrated by Russell Ayto
0-7445-9026-4
Going Up! by Martin Waddell, illustrated by Russell Ayto
0-7445-9027-2
Big Wig by Colin West
0-7445-9017-5
Percy the Pink by Colin West
0-7445-9054-X

Series consultant: Jill Bennett, author of
Learning to Read with Picture Books

First published 2003 by
Walker Books Ltd
87 Vauxhall Walk
London SE11 5HJ

10 9 8 7 6 5 4 3 2

Text © 2003 June Crebbin
Illustrations © 2003 Polly Dunbar

This book has been typeset in
Alpha Normal, American Typewriter,
Calligraphic and Helvetica

Handlettering by Polly Dunbar

Printed in Hong Kong

British Library Cataloguing in Publication Data:
a catalogue record for this book is available
from the British Library

ISBN 0-7445-9019-1